For Catherine Ann
M.B.

Library of Congress Cataloging-in-Publication Data
Burns, Maurice.
Go ducks go!
Summary: A family spends an enjoyable afternoon
racing toy ducks down the river.
[1. Games—Fiction.   2. Ducks—Fiction]
I. Brooks, Ron, ill. II. Title.
PZ7.B93737Go 1988   [E]   87-20696
ISBN 0-590-41167-5

12 11 10 9 8 7 6 5 4 3 2   9/8 0 1 2 3/9

Printed in the U.S.A.   23

GO DUCKS GO!

Story by Maurice Burns
Pictures by Ron Brooks

SCHOLASTIC INC. / *New York*

Go ducks go

Down the roary waterfall

Near the sleeping fish

Between the silent swans

Down the dark hole

Past the paper boat

Around the spinning whirlpool

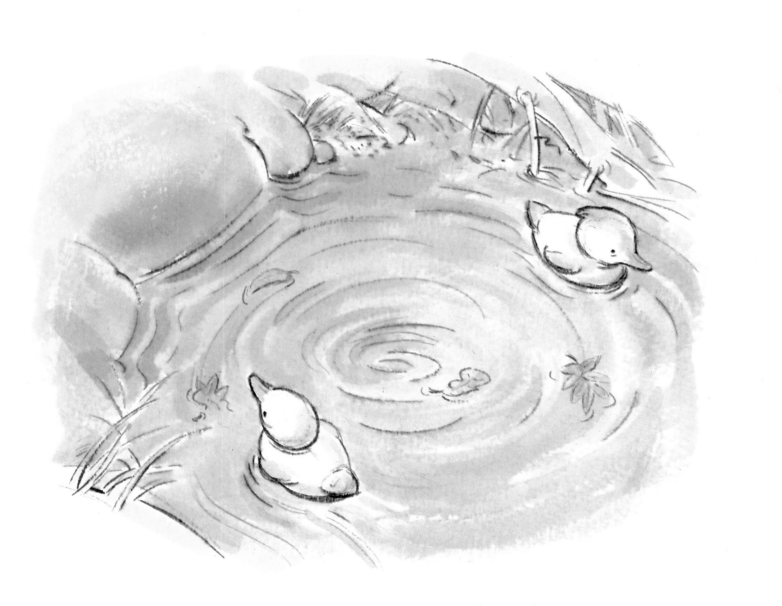

Over the bumpy stones

Under the rickety bridge

Through the fallen leaves

Along the golden sand

And back for another go